Amy's Armbands

Written by Alan Dapré

Illustrated by Sarah Warburton

Going up

"It's time to go swimming," Miss Jones said to the class.

Amy wished it was time to go home.

Miss Jones picked up a big sack and gave it to Amy. It was full of armbands.

"Don't forget to put armbands on when we get to the pool, Amy," said Miss Jones.

Amy wished she was a duck. Ducks didn't have to wear silly armbands.

On the way to the pool, a gust of wind snatched the sack out of her hand. It flew high into the air like a huge balloon.

Miss Jones was not very happy.

When Amy came home she had a big smile on her face.

"I didn't go swimming today because all the armbands blew away," she said.

"Oh dear," said Mum.

Amy saw a box on the floor.

"It's a present from your Uncle Albert," said Mum. Uncle Albert was an inventor.

Amy opened it and saw a pair of shiny armbands.

"Oh dear," thought Amy.

She spotted a small scrap of paper. It was a letter from Uncle Albert.

36 West Street
Leeds LS2 7BH

Dear Amy,

I hope you like these amazing armbands.
I made them just for you.

Love,
Uncle Albert

P.S. Don't get them wet!

"Put them on," said Mum.

Amy hoped the armbands would not fit, but they were just the right size.

Amy stretched out her arms as if she were swimming, and floated into the air.

Mum was amazed.

So was Amy.

Amy kicked her legs just as Miss Jones had shown her and floated out of the window.

"Come back!" yelled Mum. "You haven't had your tea."

Going down

Amy loved her new armbands. They were cool.

"I can see my school from up here," she said.

Mum came out of the house and looked up. Amy was now a tiny dot in the sky.

"Is it a bird or a plane?" said Miss Jones.

"No, it's Amy," said Mum, "and I wish she would come down."

"What is she doing up there?" said Miss Jones.

"Backstroke," said Mum.

Amy waved to the people in a jumbo jet. They waved back.

Then she raced a pigeon.

Amy was getting tired.

She looked down. Everything seemed so small and tiny.

Just then, a raindrop splashed on her nose...

Drip!

Then another...

Drop!

"Oh no! I mustn't get my armbands wet!" cried Amy.

It was too late.

The armbands started to shrink... smaller and smaller and smaller until they vanished with a tiny...

Pop!

Amy dropped like a stone.

"HELP!" she shouted, flapping her arms like a bird.

Down,

    down,

        down

            Amy

                dropped

                    and landed…

… on a big sack of armbands!

The next day Amy took the big sack back to school. Miss Jones was very happy. She took the whole class swimming.

Amy floated happily in the water.

It was just like floating in the air, but a lot wetter.

When Amy came home from school there was another box on the floor. It was from Uncle Albert.

Amy opened the box.

There was a shiny trampoline inside and another letter from Uncle Albert.